The Book Of Fables

The Book Of Fables

Reveries, Wanderings & Myths

by

C S Hughes

dilettante ink

ISBN 978-0-6485895-9-4 (print)
First Published in Australia by:
Dilettante Ink
PO Box 9222
Sale VIC 3850
Australia

Cover & Frontis *Ode a la Joie* © Andre Sobas
We acknowledge the people and elders of the Brayakaulang Clan of the Gunaikurnai Nation, the traditional custodians of this land, on whose Country, and by whose grace, we live and work.

Dedication

To all my princesses,
and all my ravens.

Contents

....

The Girl, The Cat, The Bird, The Stone & The Sea

She had embroidered two coats; hers threads of silvery fishing line on thick damask cloth, his dark braids of rope on rough canvas. Hers wasp narrow and ivy lost; his bale broad and ship proud. Both the same and different as any two could be.

Who was it for, her mother asked.

Someone far, far on the sea.

It is fine work though.

Thank you, mother.

Mam, on her day chair, shawled in quilts and age-softened knotwork, began an old reaping song about the maid who tied behemoth in milkweed twine. The grey light of the morning sea played ripples through the beveled window glass about her face. She was spar thin and pale as winter milk these days, but still sang the old muckle songs with crow-raucous voice.

Esbet chimed in on the last few verses.

After, Mam said, I'd had three boys by the time I was your age.

All lost to sea or lost to war now, Esbet replied, the chemise she was folding tightening in her hands.

Mam slept a while after that.

Esbet would go to the early market for the older people of the street, the fish still flailing and wet with ocean sunrise silver. Bread, cabbages, sweet potato, silver beet. The old fishermen, the stall holders, remembered her since she was small and would come in the early hours, bird voice piping amongst the shouts, to fetch back her father. By that hour drunk and flailing. He had lost his left arm to the shoulder, caught in a windlass and torn almost free when the mainsail swelled and pulled – like an angry horse in an upraising squall – he would say, recounting his story.

Caught a big one there, Esmeralda-Elizabeth, the fishwives and barrow holders would call as she dragged him homewards. He had sold his share in the boat. Spent the money in misery and carousing. He would juggle three of anything, fish, apples, cups, coals, ladles, in a precarious way, until, fumbling, all three would bruise or break or clatter on the old tavern floorboards.

Scrabbling then on his knees as much for imagined glory as for thrown silver.

She would keep a few coins, emptied from his pockets as she put him to bed, her mother weeping in the other room.

I wish the leviathan had eaten the whole of him, Mam would say as his snoring loudened. Esbet put the coins away in a cracked tea caddy, locked with a silver lock.

She still did, new coins on old. The worn-to-brass key hung on a silk ribbon he once brought, annoying against her breastbone. She would shorten the cord for it, one day.

She had been engaged once. He went to sea, a hand on a cargo scow. Never returned. She thought he must have drowned, but there was always the doubt.

There was only mother and her now, and a cat as large and angular as a demon. Lord Maconochie, the folk of the narrow street called him, doffing caps and curtsies as he prowled the tops of lichened drystone walls, eyeing birds in his repose like a yellow-eyed pharaoh Esbet had seen in a postcard once. She called "cat cat cat," and he came bounding.

One morning Lord Maconochie took the key in his mouth, made butter high on her chest, claws pinpricking through thick, layered cloth. She endured it for a while, something about the rapt stare, the husky purr, put her in mind of storm-wracked horizons. Eventually, when she felt the serrated warmth of blood bloom through the cloth of her chemise, she took Maconochie firmly in two hands, lifted and put him gently to the dully gleaming floorboards, saying, "Be away with you." He stared up awhile longer, affronted beside the turned leg of the chair, rhythmically lashing his tail, as if to silently ask, if this was really a wise choice, then bounded away through the cloud-strewn cerule of the window when the key, its loop of fabric chewed through, fell with a sound like far-off gun fire to the floor.

She thought of her brother, Adam, then, who had sent that postcard, maybe five, maybe six years ago now. *Memphis – I am going on to Caphernaum*, was all it said, and something illegible that might have been, *"learning always."*

There was no grey in her hair, it was still the colour of polished wood, but she felt grey, something in the way the brush dragged slippingly through, as if she was becoming insubstantial as lace.

The next morning she wore her velvet coat, the narwhal, the ivy, the oak of its threads speaking of long quiet hours under her fingers, cinched it with ebonized hooks and wound silk eyes, the waist tight over the sweep and fall of an earthy green skirt, donned as much for the weight of it as for the heavy morning sky. In the uncertain yellow flicker from the narrow mirror leaning above the mantle, she saw a shape like a hunting bird.

The last morning mists were still lifting from sky mottled pools, their edges fractured in the tree-shape between cobbles. Henry Wainscot, boots plashing, slowed into her path.

"Esbet," he said, licking thick lips. A rusted mail greave encased his right hand and forearm, proud flesh like barnacle trails on his left, knives in thick harness around his waist. He had the ruddy brow and sidecast glance of a man for whom such work was second nature. A smell of tobacco and *lus-nan-laogh* wafted from him as he pulled a flat cap from his head, wrenched it in his hands, finding no use for it, replaced it, covering a mat of sweat dank hair.

Esbet looked to the sweep of the cove, the village dark and gleaming as wet shingles, gulls and white caps raising.

"Mr Henry," she said, a curtsy in her voice. Steam rose from him. He seemed vast and impassable as a mire.

"Some rough work," he said, arcing his neck, indicating with sausage fingers darker stains on apron, sleeve and chest.

"Oh?" She thought of his swift knife slipping, severed fingers inching away like worms. The fish scale thing on his arm gulping amongst the blood, when there was nothing left, fat and bloated and squirming out to sea.

"I once made a wager with your Da," he said, chest thrust out, fist resting on the rust stippled pommel of a cleaver. Esbet thought of the old story, of the tailor and the seven flies.

"He boasted with his one good hand he could juggle an anchor, an apple and a throne. We didn't have a throne, but I got a cracked old chamber pot about the size of a child's head from the jakes, and I said if that would do, and if he could keep the three in the air for a few passes, he'd earn himself a handful of thrown copper."

"He was a foolish man," she said, leaning, sidling, the way ships in a headwind do.

"Aye, and still owes me." Henry creaked and jangled like a shunting train, his heavy hands closed on her shoulders, nails, callouses catching on threads. Esbet thought of a storm, and a gull, and swept under him and away. Saw him scowling behind her, frowned at the loose, pulled threads. It was ruined now; the coat. She could knot the threads back in, dab them in St Vitas to clean them, but still.

"You think winter birds eat from your hand," he shouted, and, as he gathered his loose harness, "He still owes me!"

She barely heard. By the time her fury ebbed, she was far and gone, and he was high and far behind.

The town lilted the gentle music of morning; gulls squalling or mournful around the wharf where the few fishing boats bright as toys spilled mackerel and squid; the shouts of men, warning and hauling; the jangle of horse and tack, the thrum of a motor car away over the cut, where the sun was heightening between the vying hills; the glass bell on the baker's iron bound door. It was an old house slumped as a loaf under its Marram grass thatch, made new with the scent of fresh bread and apples and flour dust each morning.

Moira was about as round and cheery as an apple herself, flour in her cheeks, butter in her hands. "You wouldn't know it to look at me now, Esbet," she was saying as she deftly wrapped loaves and baps and a rhubarb pie in striped brown paper, knotting and looping twine in drooping bows, "but when I was your age I took a boat and a train and a ferry and went as far from here as I could – to Paris where we drank green poison, and to Prague where a hussar and a sculptor duelled for my hand."

"Who won?" Esbet asked, arranging her purchases in a string bag that with each added weight stretched and stretched and stretched till almost full. She had heard the tale many times before.

"Neither – "

"Then why go?"

Moira crooked her head like a pear tree in an autumn wind.

"Do you remember the bread you ate as a child?"

Esbet remembered it well; heavy stuff made of scratchy black grains and parched brown oats, with a scrape of butter that not even a cat would lick.

"That's why."

Outside, day had cleared to an azure she had only seen in pictures. As she drifted along the esplanade, a black-tipped gull hovered in the curling breeze, not an arms length from her shoulder. It fixed her with a wise grey eye and said, *fly*, in a keening willow, before arcing out to the dunes and the cove.

"What about Mam? What about the cat?" Esbet shouted after, for all the world to hear. The bird had almost vanished amongst the schools of small white caps just off the scythe of shore. It dipped, and lifted something flailing and silver.

Lord Maconochie patrolled excitedly along the ledges of window sills and drystone walls as Esbet wended the narrow street home. "Yes, I have a sprat for you, and a sardine if you're lucky." The cat bobbed and ducked between lace curtains and terracotta pots with their ridiculous daisies.

Mam was bent as a teapot near the open fire, pinching Good Sir Henry to the broth she kept in a cauldron hung from an iron tripod above the faintly murmuring coals, a scent like mint and soft aniseed rising from the crushed leaves. She crooked up, and lowered herself in her day chair with a sigh, swaddled herself in a soft net of shawl, crooned a few murmurs of song. Esbet left her parcels of fish and bread by the tableaux of demijohns, herbs tied up in poesies, a wicker bowl of onions, on the side table, and took the silver plate and abalone shell hairbrush from the mantle, pulled a raft of her mother's white hair from the soft bristles.

"Be sure to tie that 'round a stone and throw it to the sea," Mam said, drifting off to silence as Esbet smoothed the brush through the rill of her mother's silk soft hair.

"You always had your father's hair," Mam said after a while. "If he'd grown it long he could have tied an anchor with it."

She slept then, crooked like a dove. Spoke up again, "Don't let the coals under that broth go out."

I never do, thought Esbet. She broke open a sardine, folded it back like a silver butterfly, stripped out the guts, the skeleton tree. Placed it on a cracked blue willow plate by the garden door for his lordship, who, torn between dogged and imperious looks, was silently pacing. He set to with a husk and growl, and then entirely devoted concentration.

Esbet washed her hands in soap slip and icy water. Noticed she still had on her velvet coat, the loose threads now drooping like rib bones, a smear of flour, of scale and fish guts. She dried her hands on it, back and front, back and forth, with a threshing motion. Wrenched it off so the silk wrapped eyes tore away, scuttled to the cusp of the skirting board, turned, stared accusingly, cast it to the floor where it crumpled like a dead thing, Lord Maconochie arching and bounding away.

Mam was watching, carefully now as Esbet came back to the small front parlour.

"While I've been tending that pot," Mam was saying, seemingly to someone out of sight on the opposite side of the room, "nigh on twenty years since your Da left, clouds have come and clouds have gone. They never stay, they're never the same. I've tasted that broth, but never served it, so to speak. Never savoured it."

The cat came in, sat licking a paw, surreptitiously watched.

"I think you should have a bowl, and leave."

"Who'd take care of you, Mam?"

"I'm not as weak as all that. The Mor Macrimmon comes by and plays me a summer yellow song every other day."

"He doesn't!"

"He does, and if I hadn't known him for fifty years it would almost be a scandal."

"Mam!"

Then the cat paused his grooming, cowed her with cool regard, and said, "You have a thousand smiles, girl, and only one frown. I know, I counted them one afternoon. But your face is cloudshadow – new every moment. Go to Memphis or to Tahiti, or some other far and careless place. Home will be only a little smaller when you return, but you will be someone else."

She took a bowl of broth then, savoured it, felt hands spread wide inside her, felt years unravel like the thread of a loosely knitted scarf. She wept. Raged. Took a handful of silver coins from the caddy. Smashed it so the veneer split, the ceramic gone to puzzle pieces, the coins spilled like a dragon's hoard.

Becalmed, she took her canvas coat then, from where it was carefully folded like a mourning flag, opened it like a rough, ungainly flower, felt the strength of the braids coiled on its resisting surface, shrugged into it, felt it wrapped tight around her, like a saint in armour, or a ship against a falling sun in full and roaring sail. Outside, she laughed in great sobbing breaths at the blustering sky, blew down the street like a gale, loose window shutters clattering a new rough music, clothes tearing from washing lines skirling and flailing as she passed, horses bowing and huffing and stamping, cats with flattened ears terwauling, seabirds mewling and scattering and shrieking, on to the shore where even the caplet waves for a while rose up and then stood still.

Esbet wrapped and knotted the sheaf of her mother's hair around a broad, black stone, fine grained and as opaque as sea glass, a chip on one side smoothed to a notch, secured the tangle of it with seaweed and her silk ribbon, tied, knotted and bowed. Struck back her arm like a sling.

"What kind of bird are you?" A mottled tern, swooping, asked.

The stone skipped once, twice. In sun spears and the tide's running braids, disappeared far out to sea.

Mothergrumble

Grumblemother says to chew wet leather until your jaw is strong enough to break bones and branches. She makes it out of dog. Burns the bristles off in the oily yellow flame of a handheld burner. Hollows them out. Hangs them up to dry like so many cocoons from the knotted and crowding pines. She uses willow tannins and pine rosin and the crystals left over from evaporated piss. Beetroot or dried beetle husks for colour. Murrey and blue. It has the taste of a dank and poisoned river. A taste that scalds high in the nose and throat, that can't be rid for hacking, even when you are freeing the dead, spitting marrow into clay from broken bones. When they are emptied, dried, stripped bare of meat and sinews, we break them with twelve-pound hammers, but that first break, when the soul is still hiding like a grub in the honeycomb of bone, must be broken with a brute, wordless bite.

Some – the big ones with muscles like windlasses and jaws like hatchets – she re-articulates with marrow clay and spells and silver wire. Leaves them to roam the peripheries where the forest thins to tundra, where the ice sheet thickens and buckles to a cliff-faced seawall. They hunger, those wire dogs, but can never feast, make raw work of bears and land leviathans that, drawn by the fat and sweet scents of our fires, roam too close. We wear our phylacteries, so when they come bounding up, lithe as skinned coneys, teeth bared, mouths gaping like the sea carved shore, they pull short their attack, carefully investigate with prodding noses; are we kill or kin? The bone shows through the taut stitches in the flesh here and there. Deciding the latter, the phalanx of them storms off in the wary forest silence.

Mothergrumble says if the god is roaring – furious, all is good. It lies slumped at the centre of the village like the carcase of a vast, misshapen crab, claws and guts splayed out, as if torn by vengeful birds. There are such creatures in the deeps and the wide places of the world, but this one is made piecemeal of unearthed metal.

I grunt a work song under my breath, new to such labours, forget the words, if not the rhythm, bend and shovel coke from a mound of the stuff; three scoops in quick succession through the rust and rivet port in the god's carapace. I am black with soot and sweating. The god is roaring. I slam the port to with a closed fist, feel a more insistent radiance through steel and leather. Turn the bar to lock it tight. After the length of a song wrench the thing; the hatch swings wide on its own weight, endure the fume of the god's breath. Swaying with heat, red with fire, bend to it again.

Across the clearing, beyond tangled limbs, ascending an earthern rampart to the thing's back, other youths fill the god with snowmelt from tall wooden buckets harnessed by broad leather straps to their backs. Bowing in obeisance, water pours from a spout like a tongue lolling above one shoulder. Steam plumes in geysers. We are the Dog Clan; we feed the god with water and with fire.

My sister is coming, bright in new betrothal furs, hitching the beaded leather tunic so she can clamber over tubes and pipes, the hem already black with soil. She waves and I pause. The god's entrails spread and entwine, embed in the pale craquelure adobe of our halls and homes behind her. In that loving grasp, I wonder if we are her children or her victims. Above the god, gulls with wide spread wings drift like tethered kites in the shimmering updrafts. I work at the fingertips of a thick hide glove with my teeth, wave in return, thinking of gazelles and other imaginary beasts.

Isbel shouts above the god's roar and hiss, "Mothergrumble said to bring salve and a needle." She holds these things high, beaming in triumph. As if a nascent egg had emerged, would soon hatch, pale and with its own raw heat, I have a new blister on the wing between my forefinger and my thumb.

Grumblemother says one day we will all live in Greenland - a land of figs and flowers and easy prey, seals that turn and offer their pale soft bellies, lambs sleeping in the mouths of compliant lions. The ice a far skinflint on the horizon, the shores closed to all ravening interlopers by swirling charybdis. A home for the free, the wild and artful. Till then we must strive, keep our territory and lives in marrow like misers. Still, when the day is ended, and the fire is big against the dark, when Mothergrumble drones one of her stories of hunt and truth and conquest, and we are all warm with elbows and rough felt and mead, it is pleasant enough.

Sometimes she has skin like unpeeled almonds, teeth like a laughing fox, hair a summer squall, furious and frenzied, a visage she can put on and off, perhaps in mourning, perhaps in the midst of less dire negotiations, with an upraised lip, a tilt of chin, a questing extension of the neck, as if she caught fresh magma on the air, and was, while all else around her rapt, in her nous, forewarned. Sometimes she is more plainly beauteous, wax on her skin, clay in her hair. Lips blued and eyes bright as nightshade. Matriarch and seer. Some say she is a thousand years old. I suspect she has a much more difficult provenance.

"I saw the moon hatch," Mothergrumble says, "smoke curled out like rheum from a dead man's eye. Then the mother of all leviathans ate the broken egg. The world grew dark as starless night, and as a thousand thousand times before, we thought the beast would vomit her up again, but she did not. The world swathed in silver dark grew cold. Ice encroached where no ice crept before. The seas stilled. The world slumped sidewise, as if in uncertain sleep. Grim days. Days of cries and spears and rending. Ribs like hounds, and swift." Time's fire is in her eyes. Her moving hands, fingers straining, make shapes of drifting smoke.

Tonight we must delve, for copper and for silver, into the haunted realm, the subterrane, the tomb world where the cold, and those who watch from its preserving rigidity glare in eternal hunger.

Mothergrumble says there was once a land where ash fell from the sky so fast it preserved men and women in ghost and silhouette; here, when the air coalesced to ice the souls of those entombed were similarly trapped. As we cut through the ice with saw and pick and oil burner, we must have a care not to expose a single inch of pale flesh, lest the spirit of those startled denizens escape their human-shape cocoons.

I once took a sparrow from the ice; melted around it until I had a strange kind of translucent egg, the small bird in its bandit mask preserved in the heart, struck it with the blunt blade of my hand mattock just so, so it cracked. Placed the bird inside my mouth to warm it, my cheeks puffing cold air in, warm air out. Felt the small sharp scrabble of claws, the name-song inside, opened my mouth wide, watched it fly.

We gather at the bloody pines, at the edge of the wind carved tundra, where under the sun's blear eye, in a rising breath the gnarled hides of the sentinels would sometimes crack under the cold's axe blows, the wounds seeping and filling with sap the colour of thick, translucent blood. The ice here, stained the feathery bloom of feeble sunset, was littered with the burnt bones of fallen branches. My sister, lion mask on, kicked a swathe of it high, knuckled at her sea glass eyes, in mock tears or sleepfulness, I know not which, only that her friends, similarly costumed in beast mask and raggy cloth, laughed and arched back with raised claws and growls. A few wolfs-angels, stood watch where the line of trees ceased and the nameless expanse began, arched toward the commotion, scented, turned alertly back. I thought of my own first time in the tomb world, the fear of it. Heart shouting like a drum.

"Younglings," Mothergrumble is saying, "Oldfather Winter ate the world like an egg, in one greedful gulp. It stuck in his craw, in all its gnarl and tear and grim and glamour. Now in chagrin he dreams his icy dreams. In that embryo, amongst the dead, we must go carefully, lest he wake, but – needs must. Today we give, today we receive. When the Moon left, when the Earth cooled and broke her heart, when Oldfather came ravenously to devour, she made this promise; that if we brought in barter that she may keep the bones, the bodies, the breath of our own still-lost, we may take the remnants of hers, the metal, the glass, the clay, the stone, that we may warm, and that she may preserve our dead in the sure and certain promise, when the Moon returns, of resurrection. Now to it."

Ipcre was on the wood and bear-hide stretcher, attired like us, in ghillie rags and beast mask. Out gathering hen-of-the-woods, the Oldfather's breath had come across him. We shuffled around, gathering pink stained snow, the lifefull, bloody sting of it bringing tears to the eyes, opening the nose and lungs to the cold. We scattered it on his stillness at first, then threw it in scooped handfuls. We kicked flurries, at him at each other, solemnity becoming joy becoming frenzy as he shook, as if almost alive again.

My sister threw herself on him, howled, choked it back. Her friends pulled her back. She threw cascades of snow in the air, the way the sea foams and ejects when a shoreline glacier calves; in terrible magnificence.

Calming, shivering in the aftermath, we shook off the excess. To any wandering beast we might scent and appear as a stand of stunted trees, our flanks haunted by wolfs-angels; deception and threat enough to forestall any hungering curiosity.

The ice pack is hard, our boots and gloves are embedded with dog teeth, some in rust dulled steel, some in yellow caked enamel. Our footsteps make a sound like wind scurried glaciers, like sand in a tray. Like a flock of desultory evening birds. As we proceed, the mist thicks and thins, in shallow but expansive breathing.

The ice-fog today is elusive but palpable. We have many words for it. Today's means "in the midst of joyful prayers here comes the reluctant bride". Musingly, it describes both us and our shadowed presence in the mists.

After some time - there is no time that can be accurately reckoned here - we halt where remnants of steel and machine-formed stone breaks through the earth with the ferocity and shape of a vast and tattered sailfish. We gather in the lee of its proud and decimated fin. There is a hollow whistling, a flurry, the wolfs-angels prowl and settle, are content. Dragging away the beetle wings of the cover, the entrance to the tomb world exhales the scentlessness of miasma.

We untie the bearskin from the stretcher's frame. Lash up the corners of it, making a cradle, a pouch, a sling. Tie one end of a looped hemp rope to it in a thickly wound and collared knot.

Mothergrumble nods for me and Isbel to descend. She has that stone smooth mantis mask, glass eyes like pine cones, antlers laced in snow. "Go well, Sparrowmouth, keep her safe" she says, turns aside, organising the rest on the rope to begin the process of lowering Ipcre down, as I steady the sling from underneath, while Isbel moans the wayfarer's song.

The walls are slick carved ice. Translucent in the way of unpolished glass. The shapes in the depths, and almost breaching the surface, offering promises and threats. I can feel the vibration of Isbel's song, through my gloves, through the rope supports and whalebone rungs of the ladder. As the sling blocks the light, I take Ipcre's weight on my back. Isbel hesitates a moment.

"All is well," I say. She redoubles, sings on. When we reach, in the depths, the ice tunnel with its sea dark floor and countless denizens, we rest, awaiting the others. Isbel takes off her mask for a moment. Her face quite white, webbed in tears of ice. Her breath falls to the floor in shrouds. She looks up, somehow I present her an expression, a tilt, of my own mask that offers her reassurance, that offers her comfort. A glance at the watchers behind the ice, she puts her lion mask back on.

The others arrive, suppressing hard breathing after the long descent, wary not to fix eyes with the dead. We reassemble the stretcher, undoing the bearskin's lashed corners, watch as it slowly unfolds like a flower.

A catch in Isbel's throat; she sings the rising hum again.

Grumblemother leads the way, Isbel singing following, myself bearing the front of the bier, the rest lending support around it. Ipcre's brother - to my shame I forget his name - quietly following.

I am not sure how Grumblemother decides on a suitable vault. Half scent, half sight, half seer, I suspect, but she does. We set to with our oil burners, the wall decaying in thick runnels, sluices and drops. The ice shrinking in grasping hands, pouring, refreezing in globs and elongated worms on the floor.

Soon we are through to a wall. Dismember, discard the soft chalkiness of it. We harvest the wires and pipes within, coiling it in strands and ropes. Lashing lengths of pipe in harnessed bundles on our backs.

Beyond the wooden skeleton, beyond the inner skin of crumbling plaster, is a room of alien geometries and bright coloured furnishings. There are people in the ice. In the peculiar postures of those that have not moved from their mundane pursuits in a thousand years. I, in pity, wonder, in their smooth clothes and distended grins, whether carefully removed, rather than releasing a furied ghost, if I could only open my mouth wide enough, if the beings themselves might wake in joy and in surprise.

A hand's breadth deeper in the ice is the stilled form of a bird in a cage. The sky blue of it, the sun yellow. I am almost weeping. I look to Grumblemother. She assents. I melt into the thing. Bend out the bars. Excavate the jewel in its frozen egg.

"Come now," Mothergrumble says. There is a gathering whiteness in the far depths of the tunnel. We strip Ipcre of his mask and ghillie suit. He is draped in petals and soft rosined bandages. We place his curled form in the cavity. How desperately he tries to see into our eyes.

The miasma is coming forward, swelling, growing, filling each crack and hollow and crevice with the blue solidity of new formed ice.

We wait - as is done - for the tendrils of it to fill and enclose him. Isbel is murmuring her song. As the mist takes him she throw herself into it. I reach to grapple her. It bites my fingers. I see her smile before the ice blurs and coalesces.

Mothergrumble with arms wide hustles us forwards.

"Sometimes, love," is all she says.

Outside, nearing the tall forest of home, in that strange lowering twilight, the wind dismally howling, I remember the end of an old story;

The woods are lonely, dark and deep, but I have promises to keep.

I bring the jewelled egg out from thawing against my chest. Crack the last thin shards of it. Lift the long beak of my bird mask. Place the small cold-stilled body in my mouth. Puff my cheeks in and out. The sheer, brazen ridiculousness of it. Feel the small claws scrabbling, open my mouth with a shout as wide as the sky. See the bird fly out, catch a glimmer of sun. I know not where from.

Hear its song.

Last Innings

Hambly thought; it was a colosseum, not bruised by old blood and the accretions of millennia, but of freshly cleaned bone, refined by an aeonic process of repetition, to a pure and shadowless white, not the pristine white of Christmas, nor the phantom-white of a suddenly billowing gas flame, but the white of masks and ash and funerals, now smeared by the shapes cast under a lowering sun of men brought to a halt, and in the throes of catching from the blue air, the ghosts of their breaths.

The dogs, in their traces, perhaps more sensibly, slumped to the hard packed ice, dark stoic eyes looking expectantly from below brows arched in fine crystals of snow, for a morsel.

"No sign of the *Borealis*, Captain?"

Captain Combridge stood on the lip of the depression, gazing out at the sharp-toothed field of blue-white shards in the twilit seas of Egg and Chicken Bay. The lowering, eyelet sun broke through the enclosing overcast for a moment, as if just to light on him with some sort of honeyed blessing. He'd allowed his beard to grow into the fierce affront of some mountain prophet, but still carefully waxed the architecture of his broad moustaches every day. Despite privation, he remained broad as a rock, knuckling at his lip with hard, strangler's hands.

He was, in Hambly's estimation, a lunatic. Inspired, yes. A lunatic nonetheless. He'd brought one sled and team of twelve just for furniture. A roll top desk, a small walnut pianoforte from Salarzin of Leipzig, decorated in a Rabelaisian manner with scenes of fauns and maidens in risqué frolic, that once belonged to Frederick The Great.

"We must bring civilisation with us to God's abandoned places," he'd said, quite seriously. The pieces were now spread out over the 500 mile extent of their route, re-supplying camps and base stations from Mt Hope to McMurdo Sound. When they'd had to leave it behind, the remaining, half starved dogs no longer able to bear the weight, on a comb of ice like the encrusted bones of some long petrified behemoth, he'd sat there delicately picking out a Bach etude, the *Aria da Capo*, fragile as ice in those big, murderous, bloodless hands, tracks of tears frozen on his face.

Of course he'd left the first hand, Carothers, the astronomer, Zygo, and the Darwinian biologist whose name always escaped him at other nameless and vacant coordinates with scant prayers and no ceremony, except a few, brief jottings of arc and minute and latitude on the map. At the blasted site of the pianoforte, after his impromptu performance, he declared the formation, forever, for all men and and all time, *The Goldberg Wasteland*.

"I've become familiar -" he was saying as he turned, interrupting Hambly's musings, "to the point of contempt - with ice and snow in all its furied devilry, but I have never seen such as this. Ugly, dead, leprous. A whited sepulchre if ever I saw one."

"Nor I, Sir."

He checked the map once again, the squirrelled lines as indistinct as an old hand's tattoos, folded the waxed sheets, replaced lovingly in their shagreen binder, consulted compass, chronometer, sextant, each carefully returned to its shaped receptacle, hidden again about the lumpen scarecrow of his person. Calculated against the tables in his mind, said, "Nevertheless, as the man said - better three hours early, than three minutes late. There's an easy route down the cliff face when she arrives, bear up, Hambly, home by June."

"The men are flagging, Captain. I'm not sure they'll last three hours." The dozen or so survivors, who had stumbled blindly through nine days of blizzard, another four of blinding, numbing, interminable whiteout, slumped or lay like rags and debris against the spars of sleds. Nothing left to show of their humanity except the strained expulsions of their whited breath. The few malamutes rested warily, in the lee of an area of low stepped obsidian rocks, warming noses between extended paws.

Combridge considered a moment. A few stray penguins had returned from the sea, filed in twos and threes up the narrow path from the rock and ice-bound shore below, gathered in their rookeries amongst the black stones at the edge of the shallow oval depression. Watched with small, hard eyes from behind burlesque feathered masks. Issued harsh and elegant and raucous warning cries.

"You know what the Major would have done?"

Major Ayers had lead them a hundred miles off course, into a blizzard and a mazy no man's land of shards and shadowed shapes, through privation and unending whiteout, to the edge of a kind of madness, then shot his arm off with an elephant gun in what could only be described as a hunting accident. He'd brought a brace of them. Hambly wasn't sure why. Walruses? Penguins? Russians? They'd eaten the Major. Well, technically they'd fed him to the dogs, then some immeasurable days later, in the peculiarly isolating glow of a fire made of a broken up sled and a small, elegant chinoiserie, they'd eaten two of the remaining dogs. To Hambly, for reasons he wasn't willing to explore, that seemed almost the same. Except the Major's head. Combridge had insisted on keeping that, carefully wrapped in strips of waxed canvas and sewn into a leather bag, to honour at home in England. Hambly imagined it, the pained, surprised look still about the mouth and patrician nose, mounted on the smoke stained, mahogany panelled walls of a dining hall at the *Royal Expeditioner's Society*, amongst the disgruntled tigers and dismayed gazelles, with others of its ilk.

"I don't know, Sir. Cricket?" Hambly proffered, mouth, too late, twisting. Irregardless of their folly, it was ill to speak so of the dead.

"Exactly!"

Combridge banged his hide wrapped forearms together, creating a dirgesome but penetrating beat.

"You men," he said. "We have dragged ourselves through this sorry hell, through the heart of emptiness, born all the contempt it threw at us. Lost good men and good dogs to its hunger. Though some may say we have fallen, failed, I say nevertheless; we have made sure the path for those that must inevitably follow. We have raised the flag, in this blighted place, as is our tradition. Now is not the time to rest, on our laurels, on our weary haunches – *but arise*. We shall show this land that we are far beyond defeat. *Pugnasse, lusimus, vicimus*, as great Caesar may have said. Form yourselves up, while we await the *Borealis*, in honour of our fallen, in defiance of that which would deny us, in keeping with our tradition, I think, a game of cricket. England versus Australia, we'll show them what kind of men we are, or may the Empire fall."

Knudsen, who was removing the dogs from their traces, getting them settled, the only busy figure in the vast and echoing landscape, was the first to speak.

"Canadian, sir," he muttered, in his bluff way, from the depths of his bearskin parka, feeding scraps to the impatient huskies. After a pause proffered, by way of further explanation, "don't know cricket."

"It's rather like baseball, except vertical," said Underwood, a spry young ship's hand who'd signed on the outbound run from Hobart, and offered to remain with the party when a musher had become ill with appendicitis mid-voyage and been left ashore in a doctor's care at Macquarie Island Station. "Cricket mad, I am. I have the Major's bat in my pack. The Major said to me, 'If anything should happen to me, my boy, see this old willow is returned to the halls of Rutherford - where I first played.' But I'm sure he would have wanted us, in these circumstances, while we wait, to play."

"Come on you fellows. We can position sleds here and here," said Hambly. He didn't much care for sports, *per se*, but could see the value in keeping the men active, busy, distracted. The practicalities of organising things, was, however, his *metier*. "Backs facing each other, as wickets."

The men roused themselves up. Lumbered about, unloading the sleds of their remaining tarpaulined packages. An oval mirror. A typewriting machine. A Chippendale dresser. A three-quarters life-size statue of Queen Victoria, enthroned with lions, in the neo-classical style. Various indiscriminate boxes. The sleds were arranged. Creases drawn with the blunt hook of a whaler's knife in the hard pack snow - though the pitch was somewhat shorter - the regulation four feet from the wicket.

"Uneven numbers, Sir. We have five Australians, seven English, one Irish, one Kiwi and our Canuck." Underwood reported to Hambly, as tasks completed, the men gathered up.

"England versus the colonies, I think," said Combridge, returning from his outlook on the outthrust lip of the ledge. Whilst looking out to the vast grey blue. Empty but for sea birds and scintillations, and trailing into the distance, the sparse white tips of icebergs in their convoys, he had observed proceedings nevertheless.

"Knudsen as umpire. Knudsen, you are to observe closely and make determination on the rules of play. The object is of course for a player to score points whilst at bat, by striking the ball to the boundary to earn six points should the ball reach the boundary - in the vicinity of those penguins there (a large crowd of penguins had gathered by now, chattering and preening, eyes painted for war), four points if it should reach the boundary along the ground. The batsman may also earn points by running between wickets if the ball should fall short of the boundary. The opposing player to strike them out, by hitting the wicket with the ball whilst the batsman is outside of the safe zone, behind the crease."

"I'm sorry, Sir. It doesn't make much sense to me. The only sport I follow is the Iditarod," Knudsen said, scratching at the lead dog's - Shirley's - brindle ear with a thick-gloved hand. The dog also seemed somewhat confused.

"Think of it as an act of invasion and colonisation, Knudsen. The batsmen are the native people, guarding and holding claim to their territory. There isn't enough of them to hold their entire territory, so when they fend off an advance by the invading forces - the thrown ball - they must run up and down to demonstrate that they do, in fact, claim all of the territory, rather then just the safe space near the wicket. Meanwhile, the encroaching colonists surround them in the field of play, occupying and making claim to the outer territories, whilst those with authority, the crown, the state, the government, the armed forces, the lords and land owners, are the bowler, they continuously pitch balls - launch attacks - on the natives in order to dispossess them."

Knudsen, rather obstinately, Hambly thought, continued to look confused.

"Iditarod is just a dog race, Captain. It don't involve pitching balls at natives."

"Indeed. I will advise on the finer points and technicalities as we proceed."

"Speaking of balls, Sir," Hambly said to Combridge, "we don't seem to have one."

"Does anyone have a ball in their pack? A cricket ball, a tennis ball, a golf ball, a child's India rubber bouncing ball? Anything round will do."

There was a certain amount of shrugging, patting of parka pockets and half-hearted milling about before Underwood said, "There, on your sled, Captain. Right at the top. It's a bit over large, but will certainly do the job." There was indeed a round object in pride of place on the Captain's sled, secured by straps, about the size of a small football, in yellowing leather, a curve of neat criss-cross stitches on one side.

"That, Underwood, is the Major's desiccated head, which we are returning, to England, for burial."

"Play called off due to importunate circumstances, Sir?" Inquired Hambly.

"Cricket mad, like me, Sir," said Underwood. "I'm sure the Major wouldn't mind. For the men, Sir. For the Empire!"

Hambly shuffled over to retrieve the object in question. From one angle, the row of stitches rather looked like a disapproving frown. From the other, an uproarious smile. It made the whole enterprise seem somehow, cheapened, dishonourable. As if they had come here to raise flags and build roads, but had, instead, defecated and disguised their filth under clean, white snow. Still, after weeks and miles of privation, cricket was about the only thing that made sense.

"Somewhat awkward. It does have a rather good heft, Sir."

"Does anyone have a coin, for the toss? " It seemed the Captain, through the moment's chagrin and glory, had also acquiesced.

"We can use my old compass, Sir, " said Hambly. "It's broken anyway."

The teams formed up around Combridge, Knudsen, Underwood and Hambly as he tossed the small brass disc flashing into the air. It landed face up, the blued steel needle spinning wildly, before settling with a heave and twitch, SSW on Combridge and the English team.

"Look, Sir, the lights "

In the grey irk, above the bleary sun, sheets and waves of blue and pink and sinister green flickered and spread in coruscations thrown across the sky.

Even the penguins were silent for a moment.

"It's as if…some vast and ancient gods looked on," said Underwood, reverently taking the ball, feeling it's width and weight, the downturned seam, it's unusual indentations.

Combridge was before the wicket, champing at the ground with the tip of the bat. Knudsen stood at the bowler's end. Shirley by his side, still rather flummoxed. Hambly there too, as the alternate batsman, crouched over, ready to run.

The fielders spread about the arena, bent over, gloved hands together, scarecrow figures indistinct in a new upswirl of snow. The few remainders of the English team gathered on a high point by the ledge, the green light in their eyes and faces, watching rather disconsolately.

Underwood took a few, short, brisk steps up to the wicket and with a firm, compelling, sure and true overarm motion, bowled.

The ensconced head flew in a long, downwards arc, wobbling slightly. Combridge took two determined steps forward, raising the bat back at almost shoulder height. The penguins shrieked. Willow hit leather with a resounding crack. The ball propelled through the air towards the perimeter of sky and sea beyond the ledge. Shirley gave chase, and leapt.

It seemed the gods had stood and roared. With an immeasurable sound, somewhere between complaint and too-close thunder, a crevice cleaved along the landward perimeter of the oval depression, the wedge-shaped forward ledge of the glacier calved, crumbled, slid down into the roil and tumult seas below.

The penguins, beyond the boundary of black rocks where they and other sea birds had kept their rookeries for millennia, raised their flippers to their faces against the sudden flurried snow.

Nearby, sceptre in one hand, orb in the other, attended by lions in repose, her empty marble eyes already hazed by surface fractures forming in the increasing cold, Queen Victoria looked on.

Epilogue

(A Wireless Telegraph Report From The Ice Breaker, *Borealis*, Ross Sea, Antarctica, May 4th, 1913)

We waited three weeks at the appointed coordinates, an unnamed rockbound cove on McMurdo Sound. Crew somewhat restless. Blizzards and storms sighted south east, inland. Rising seas. Coming in to that season where the ice shelf breaks up, making encounters with icebergs an increasing hazard.

With no sign of Major Ayers' shore party, after discussions amongst the ship's officers, it was determined that it would be safest to depart.

Our prayers with Ayers, Combridge and men, in the hope that sighting the extremities of weather, they remained at the Shackleton Inlet base camp.

Causing no little wonder, shortly after our departure, at the head of another ice and rock bound bay, approximately three and half nautical miles from the aforementioned coordinates, the watch reported a woman accompanied by beasts on the distant cliffs. Further observation through the ship's telescope revealed nothing more than some unusual formations of rock and snow, however, much to our surprise, soon thereafter, we discovered a sled dog, and a cricket bat, and another, somewhat more gruesome object, that the dog was loathe to be parted from, adrift on a berg, details of which I will not enter into this record.

C. W. Roberts
Captain
H.M.S.S. Borealis

Carpe Diem

Mists swirl and clear, revealing an elaborate hearse, all ebon wood and brass finials; railings, bearing within glass panelled sides, a small white coffin, surmounted by flowers, preternaturally bright in the fog of pre-dawn.

The horse, in its traces, is of the pantomime variety. Baggy skinned, cartoonishly dappled, and wearing a crumpled top hat, its bent ears poking through the brim.

Leaning against the tall spoked wheel of the carriage. Still, shadowy figures.

The dawn brightens, a glow grey through the slowly thinning mist reveals stones and statuary, rising serried rows, diverse but orderly. Upon the hill, the yellow claw-headed shape of a digging machine. Distant, beyond bordering pines, the outlines of carnival structures, a Ferris Wheel, and other less familiar machinery, shadowed, still and stark upon the horizon.

The sky the colour of the space between dreams brightens of a sudden. The two figures are revealed. Pink faced in the cold, much of a muchness.

Resplendent in funereal confection. Gleaming black ribbons. Tall silk top hats. Kid gloves. Pressed three-quarter coats. No more, no less. Vests trousers shoes. Black on black on black. Even their eyes like polished coal.

Black strings, almost invisible, extend from our poor players, up into the infinite.

"And today?" asks Edgar.

"The quieted machinery of joy," says Mr Euphrates. He drops a fag end to the ground. Grinds it under the toe of a gleaming leather shoe. Gravel scrapes. Birds hush for a moment.

"And today," he says, in a voice neither here nor there.

"Today we bury a child," says Edgar. He turns up his collar, against the cold, for a moment. For propriety he turns it down again.

"Hm." A sudden gust soughs through the silent moment.

"The trees, the way they are swayed and whispered by the wind, and suddenly still, do you not find it...fearful and ominous?" Edgar's voice is also quieted.

"I have no fear of them," says Mr Euphrates, matter-of-factly.

"You have been at this work too long, then, if you do not find, on a morning when we bury a child, that the noble pines and bent-statured oaks grieve the sadness of the wind."

"No. No. It is not that I am inured past mystery, so wearied by routine that I am dumb to the significance, so read, so spoken. It is only, I am grown beyond fearing."

"So you are an old soldier," says Edgar, and in voice fading "bloodshed has you death's maid of honour, laying the mudded train of earth upon those who wed the great polygamer, in requiem for the nameless, the faceless, left at the altar by the dissolute avowal of your rifle."

"I was a soldier, yes," replies Mr Euphrates. "I left I do not know how many unknown, unburied, open eyed yet sightless to the sky. But those I inter today I do not bury in recompense to the unburied of yesteryear. I have known killing but I do not know death."

"Today we bury a child. Grievous," says Edgar. He shakes his head. "The trees cry. You will not respect and fear."

Mr Euphrates nods. "We all know the shell game is a trick, but the many of us still choose to be deceived."

"A hero of wars past, who, in his wisdom no longer gambles." says Edgar, perhaps with a respectful sarcasm.

"No." says Mr Euphrates. "And again, No. Before the war, I suffered *grande mal*. The seizures would throw me to the earth, trembling. I thought, then, that was like death. (A pause of denial.) After the war, I do not know by what vicissitudes, for I suffered not the slightest physical wound, at a time when I was responsible for, well, one shell game or another, I experienced a seizure in which I no longer trembled, I no longer swooned as of death. I feared. A fear gripped my ankles, my viscera, my throat. I ran until I could not. Feaaar. Blinding, sweating, adrenal. You understand? Lacking any object of terror with which the mind could even begin to grapple. The site of my epilepsy had altered to where reside the base emotions, the temporal lobe. I knew fear, white hot and unconscionable."

"You must have known it was the epilepsy...your previous experience," avowed Edgar.

"It happened thrice before I realised."

"Thrice!"

"Thrice," says Mr Euphrates (with finality, then a pause.) "I cannot recall the experiences to you."

"You lived then, in fear of the fear."

"The fear of the fear was a harbinger, a goad, a constant, ominous foreshadow of the unreckoned force of the moment of seizure."

"So now?"

"I was consumed by Nepenthe. Later, other drugs. They weakened and wearied my body, my youth. The potential of recurrence tormented me, mind and soul. I spent years, how many, I no longer know, in fear of fear."

"You are no more in fear of fear," says Edgar, a conclusion like straw.

"I turned to the grave-work, at first perhaps, driven by the necessity of a choice; to escape or endure. I was wracked then. Gluttonous with heat and venom and night. In these memorious gardens, amongst the many, remembered only in moments, only as ciphers of moments, and for that, perhaps, unremembered but in stillness, yet speaking, a solemnity, calming as autumn evening, settled upon me. I chose, and stopped the drug. Soon thereafter I strengthened, in body, in spirit. The fear had cauterised the epilepsy, the epilepsy the fear."

"You without fear. These interred ciphers, as you call them, silent in sepulchres. Speaking only in remembered voices or the deceit of speech given them on living tongues. Without the respect, the godly respect, born of fear, the lives they speak through memory become the acts and dialogues of poppets, of marionettes. You must fear and offer due respect."

"You presume to know fear? Your strings are showing. This fearing you suppose invokes respect is no more than the cowering of a cur before its master, of a man before his. It is to placate the living, to submit obeisance to every institute that holds him, that he erroneously holds as his. It is to play of their lives a shell game, in which choice is denied, the prize is palmed, they are judged ill or good, summarily sentenced nevertheless. This respect is more ignorant than death. I do not call the dead, for dead men tell no tales, nor honour them, but give them peace which is their due. Beyond fear, how can I do otherwise?"

(A pause, the men stretch, yawn and gaze around.)

"The day warms," says Edgar.

"Forgive my momentary tone of anger, to speak in defence of the unvoiced, is a challenge to which my passion rises."

"It is understandable. In debate, strong words are exchanged and easily forgotten. Your undertaking is indeed a challenge; for, truly, is not to speak for another, to speak their voice as your own; the unvoiced cannot speak. Your words have not been spoken."

"Perhaps, I have not spoken my words."

"Nor theirs."

(Both feign ignorance of the others' presence, for a moment, adjusting the fine black strings, glinting in the brightening day, that rise vertically from knee, wrist and head, into the blue.)

"Who then is speaking," says Mr Euphrates.

"Who is speaking?" asks Edgar.

"Who speaks?" enquires Mr Euphrates.

"Speaks?" Edgar queries.

"Who?"

Both laugh.

Edgar acknowledges with a gloved hand the conveyance within the bedecked and glassed carriage. He says, jaw clacking, "This one. The coffin was made small. The mother could not pay for another. The mortician broke the child's legs to cramp her in the box. There is little peace in that."

"Still flesh knows no discomfort. Yet here we are with all our finery. Do you find peace in grave- work?"

"Ah, so so. It is work as much as prayer is labour. I am diligent and respectful in both. Formerly, I have butchered, I have worked machineries and mills, I have driven taxis. I am concerned of the news and pray for the starving. I feast on the sabbath. I honour my wife and do not understand my children. It is life, goodly ordered. Quarter of a half, half of a quarter."

"I wonder for whom the wind grieves. Sometimes it seems the living more than the dead."

"Once I too was a doubter. I doubted all things, and lived in uncertainty. I suppose it was doubt lead me to this work, where I found the inevitable."

"Now you are sure, Edgar?"

"As the sky is blue. Certain."

"Then you were certain of your uncertainty?"

"This is glim, all bridled and relenting. What a way of speaking."

"Calm, calm. It is certainly beyond doubt that you were in doubt."

"Well, I suppose that must be, for in doubting doubt, it would leave open that I was not in doubt, which was certainly not so."

"Doubtless. A possibility as open, as welcoming and as certain as the grave," concludes Mr Euphrates.

"Now *your* strings are showing."

"Pardon," says Mr Euphrates. With a flourish, a flight of doves from his sleeves, his strings are gone, but for a glimmer.

They look to the distance, don their hats, then proceed to open the carriage doors.

"Hold. The procession comes. This morning we bury a child."

"It is time. The sun is well risen."

A Tower Rose

Upon a time a tower rose from an expanse of bracken and tangled thorn that spread from broken storm wracked cliffs to impassable bluffs of mountain. The mountain peaks shone black with granite and white with snow, and yet the clouds around their tops could not surpass those that swirled around the tower.

Of slag and shingle, swathed in mist, from the spun glass cage atop, each morning as the sun lit yellow, a still clear voice sang out. Birds in the tangle below shrugged their wings and rose from their nests and ascended the great height carrying fruit and seeds and flowers, and sometimes forgetting themselves in zeal or spell, a grub or spiny caterpillar or clawed earwig. The girl in the tower awaited their bounty and accepted it all with good grace. She separated seed and fruit and all good things from the worms of the earth. These the girl fed to a great golden parrot that meandered about the filigree chamber waddling in a manner from perch to ledge to rail that denied its great dignity and stately beauty.

As she fed it it would cry in a raucous balloo,"Girl with the voice worth its weight in gold, when will you sing for me?"

And the girl would reply, "Tell your cruel Master, when he tells me my name, I shall sing for him, but not before, and never again."

The great golden parrot would gnash its ebon beak, glare a ruby eye, upstart in a manner that belied its dignity and fly off in a frenzy of wings and squawks to relay the answer.

The girl would spend her day singing, and where each note lilted, and each trill fell, spun glass would turn to spun gold, each bug that harked now turned a golden claw, each bird that flew too close now fell with a golden wing.

Upon return the parrot would screech, "Though your voice be worth its weight in gold, my master has no name for you until the day you die." And the girl's golden song would fall silent, big glistening tears would run down her face as she watched from the balcony, as the sun sank and the stars glittered, and her tears fell through the night, capturing colours from reflection and becoming spun glass with a sound like the ringing of small weary bells.

She had lost count of her days in the tower. She had seen winter come to the distant peaks in shrouding storm, and summer in gleaming snow and stone upon the pinnacles six times. After the first she had determined to throw herself from the balcony to the rock and thorn of the thicket below, but the parrot stood before her with upraised wings, buffeting the air so that she fell back. There was something dreadful about the night. When she threw herself from the balcony in the depths of the night, when the parrot was away about its master's business, into the darkness, the glittering stars, the tower catching darkness in glass and gold and polished stone shingle, and she thought she would be torn on bramble, crushed on stone, consumed by the gnawing mouths of the small grave creatures of the earth, amid the rushing air there was again a great buffeting, of many wings, and the many small birds that brought her food and solace in the mornings lifted her up to her prison again, their small voices chiding.

Reconciled to live, when she sang her song the following day, even the clouds turned gold. The golden clouds scant across the sky like great ships, and when they fell as rain upon the stony ground of a far distant land, the people there rejoiced. Not only did they fill their pockets with the wealth of kings, golden fruit sprang up from the ground where the rain had fell, corn and pumpkins and butternuts and lemon trees and yellow grapes from parched ground. The people rejoiced, except for one.

A prince of that land, as he walked with his betrothed as gold fell from the sky and bloomed everywhere from the earth, but the only gold he saw was that of her eyes. "I have of you this," and he placed a silver tube to his eye and looked upon her joyous face,"from a wizard of a distant land a collide-o-scope, which makes of your face a gem and a flower, and a moment that I may keep. If you look upon me from the other end, I also am kept by the gem at the heart of the thing."

"Ah my love that is a marvel. What I have for you is ordinary, I have made from the finest beeswax a candle for our wedding night, with rich scented oils and 'erbs, as the common folk do, and as my mother taught me. As it burns through the night, as it releases rosemary for constancy, saffron for fortune, rose-apple for fruitfulness, ginger for long life, poppy for peacefulness, and others of what I cannot tell, so blessings and blessings will be upon us." She placed it in his hands.

"Oh that is a marvel beyond the artifice of any wizard. Until that night, I will guard it safe." They clasped hands and their warmth lit each other. Then a great golden feather swept from the sky falling true like an arrow, and pierced her heart. She fell to the ground, a sound like glass breaking on her lips. Gold vines entwined her, flowers like bells unfurled in a moment, drank silver from her cheek, withered. He fell to his knees beside her, gasping great sobs as the rain pelted, until gold filled the chambers and the fibres of his heart, and his heart froze.

"Oh prince we would weep, but we are all princes now, where there was a lord there is now a duke, where there was a duke there is now a prince, where there was a prince there is now a king, where there was a king there is now an emperor," his people said, servant, soldier, smith and suzerain, and scoffed, and raised each a glass of golden wine.

"Where there was demanding soil, there are now bones," the prince said. "Where there was companionship, song, joy, beneath these ripe fruits, there is gleaming stone."

"Father, I shall find from whence this boon came."

He lay his betrothed in the earth, strapped the hard golden feather to his belt as a sword, turned his hat toward the horizon and his back toward the sun, filled his pockets full of the gold of the sky and set forth.

Mikhaèl (for that was his name) followed the morning, the sun filled his eyes until his shadow disappeared under his feet, and in the afternoon he followed the golden road. From town to village to small holding and croft where pumpkin and marrow grew in abundance and the people drank yellow wine. They cheered and jeered him on his way, as he asked, "Did the clouds sail hence, did the sky fall here?"

"Oh yes the sky fell here. Stay and revel," they would say, for they saw his father's face was on every coin, but he refused their sour wine and sharp relish, taking only a little rice and roast fowl.

"Sing me a song so sweet it will break my heart and make me weep tears of glass then I will stay in your golden town." Mikhaèl would say to each jewel bedecked mayor or gold clothed lord who offered the hand of their sunny maiden daughters.

The maidens would sing, and the minstrels and choirs, milk maids and milksops, and good wives and broad wives, but it sounded like braying and boasting and a hullabaloo, raucous and rowdy not a note sung true.

The prince walked on until the soles of his shoes wore through and his beard grew long. Now the golden road was sparse, dank villages of tumble down shacks with hard eyed folk guarding the last withered fruit on a leaning lemon tree or thorny vine.

"Oh our gold we grasped until it turned black, a blight swells upon the tree, its bounty moulders, our sour wine is vinegar, and all our glad songs sting our eyes, but for a little gold we'll tell you what way the clouds came, the golden clouds you seek, that brought such hail, swollen with sunshine gathered high in the place between the winds and the waves."

So Mikhaèl emptied his pockets of precious dust, but when the townsfolk had gathered it up their Captain in his tarnished buttons only said, "There." Indicating with clubs and mattocks a stony path, a dark path, the trees a tangle, the earth a mire. "We have your bright gold and you have a dark road where none go, where all are lost of poison thorn and sucking bog where dwells a beast, a bone breaker, a ghoul, an oger, a render who will make whistles of your spindleshanks and play his dirgeful tune."

"The valley between the winds and the waves lies just beyond this Gravewood?"

"Aye, but you shall never find it."

Mikhaèl set light foot to the path. The air and the silence were chill, but for a distant soughing that stirred the miasma under the thick canopy of dank and sunless leaves, the ill green nearest black. The tangled vines and broken stems turned from black to grey to bone white where they jutted from greasy loam and bitter yellow moss. In the widowed dark, as the air sucked through the holes on each carved shank, a note added to a keening, mournful tune.

Then a great voice said, "You have danced this far, you shall dance no farther. My song of broken bones is not a merriment for your dancing feet, it is a paean to make you weep, a mourn to your grave, whence your hollowed bones will join my sad orchestra."

"My heart is gold as cold as stone my bones will never sing. I have danced this black path to your tune and never sunk in mire, so the piper will pay as fate and guest right does decree, I have danced until your silence."

The creature then stood from his throne of broken bones and piled gold, in the small vale that was his domain, where all paths ended. A frown shortened the fish-white slab of his brow. The laurel of finger bones and thorns and leaves upon it tipped as his eyes sank in thought. His mouth a hard shelf like a cracked sepulchre, its hollow crowded with tilted grave stones and noisome exhalations pressed tight like a good woman's scold. It hitched its robe of swathed moss and stepped forward, great oaken arm sweeping in a gesture at once cordial and beyond refute.

"I hold you have danced my Gravewood until by chance the breath that played my pipes grew silent, and I acknowledge there is no song I may extract from your cold bones even if I were to break them in defiance of fate and the law of guests and pipers, but here there is no path to the place you seek, only I in my great stone shoes may traverse these lands, unstung by grasping thorn, unswallowed by ravenous earth. Your shoes have neither lace nor sole. Their leather has perished. There is nowhere left for you to dance. You cannot walk in my great shoes. Turn whence you came." The oger turned.

"Oh my feet are calloused, my soles are thin, but I have yet a few steps in me," cried Mikhaèl, and one, two, three, leapt upon the oger's back, grasped the crown on its brow like a rein and pulled until the circlet sat harness across the bridge of the beast's nose, its hooks pierced the monster's cheeks. It started to claw and flail and Mikhaèl shouted, "If I only pull a little more on this bridle, the jags of it will hook out your eyes, then how will you make the pipes for your pretty tunes? I mayn't walk in your shoes of stone, but where I whither, you shall stride."

"You may ride me to that place you seek, but ere you dismount I will break your bones and suck their marrow, and though they may not sing, that golden heart you bear in your chest will make such a pipe as to command the birds from the sky!"

"Oh grim steed, ere I dismount I will have your dark eyes out on these thorny hooks, they may show my path, they may not, but afore you break me, we shall see. Onward, toward the sun." Mikhaèl pulled a little on the rein, and the oger set forth, lifting each great stone shoe and placing it steadfast before him, crushing vine and bracken, pulling up from the sucking mire as easily as a fly trudging on spilled treacle.

The Gravewood fell away, and soon mountains of black stone asleep in white rose high into a cold sky.

"This is my mother's country," said the oger. "She will make of you not a song, nor even bones or peaceful dust, but a thing of black stone high and alone, worn away every moment by scouring winds and scoring ice, for an age upon an age. And I also."

The monster halted as the slope now canted up to the ridged stone back. Here a keening song was torn from every huddled stone. "My mother's song, a hard and endless tune. I will make with you a bargain. You will not take my eyes, so that I may depart and not wander blind in this vault, and I will not break your bones or make a whistle of your golden heart. I hear it is called a bargain and is something men make."

"I will make that bargain, for a wreath and an eye," said Mikhaèl, and leaped from the oger's back, twisting the crown just so, that it pulled forth one dark eye from the monster's head.

"Oh, oh!" cried the oger, in a voice no longer cavernous, but small.

"Quiet lest you mother hear, and make of you that dread stone, etched beyond time and endurance. This small marble is a trifle by comparison, and this diadem a trinket, a surety of our bargain that I will return to you, if you no longer rend bones in the Gravewood, but only bury them, if you clear the thorns and bridge the mire. Make your song from wood and string."

"You have sat upon me a burden. Without an eye I cannot carve, without a crown I cannot rule, without a rule my forest pipes cannot play, without that tune I cannot sing. My mother's song of stone is hard, but a bargain with man is the cruelest thing."

"Monster you may find that service to a burden is not a chain but a song."

"And you man, up in that hard cold place, the peaks you must pass to enter the vale between the winds and the waves, may find my mother." But there was a look about the monster's maw of stone that of a sudden fit together, from the squared jaw a refrain muttered, sounding like grit and gravel, "Tear the vine, lash the trunk, shape the boards, box the bones, make the bridge."

Mikhaèl placed the crown upon his head, with its gruesome gem still looking this way and that. He bound moss to his feet, thick and golden, and set upon the black stone flanks of the mountain.

The mountain rumbled, stones tumbled, ice creaked. Mikhaèl sang, "It is I your stone fleshed son, come to call as a good son does, do you not know my thorny crown, do you not know my gleaming eye?"

Then the mountain quietened. After toiling up through scree, and granite and ice and obsidian, hands scratched by stone and pink with cold, breath snatched in gasps from his lips, he neared the peak where the winds tore at him and tried to cast him down.

"No son of mine, not stone of flesh. Why do you climb upon my breast, I am the rock and the hard place, I am the teeth of the wind, the only succour I have for you is a precipice," came Mother Stoneheart's voice, soft upon the wind.

"When you look upon the shining coal from whence the world is made, love for me will hold you still and my voice will weary you for an aeon."

"Each day of my long journey I have stared into the gold of the sun, your black shining heart is dull to me, my golden heart is still and belongs to another."

She harried him with a gale, but the moss on his feet held to the stone as he staggered, and where he fell in the lee of the stone husks of those she had captured and carved for a thousand thousand years, they sheltered him.

Then the ice came down in great sheets, thrumming and moaning, implacable, a crystalline surf breaking stone and statue before it, nothing but white in its wake.

Where the husk of an unfathomable beast tore and broke, a black fissure opened in the blacker stone. Mikhaèl entered, a curiously warm exhalation, warm with the salt of blood.

"I am Mother Stoneheart, Mother Stone, Mother of Mountains, I am the coal that does not burn, the ice that does not melt, I am the world's withering, the feaster of shadows, you think of me as the heights, I am the depths, though I enfold you in my cold bosom, you shall find no comfort. Welcome."

The stone walls creaked and shuddered, Mikhaèl held aloft the thorny circlet with its ugly fruit. "Here is your mighty son's crown and his dark eye, destroy me and you crush them also." The walls narrowed and narrowed with a great rending, but when they touch either side of the crown they stilled.

Ice closed over the mouth of the crack and there was dark, and silence.

After a time, the wall of ice behind was the blue of night. No stars gave promise. Mikhaèl kindled a flame from his tinderbox and lit his candle. The flame burned bright, golden and blue, but would not melt the ice. His blade scored the dark, but would not cut it. The smell of beeswax dispelled the foetid air and the candle flickered. Here in the cold dark, enveloped in the weak, wavering glow, it promised a way out; or perhaps it was the breath from the heartbeat of the Mother of the Dark, Mikhaèl walked ere she slumbered but nevertheless watched from the edge of dream.

The circle of yellow light picked out the edges of broken black rock walls like layered faces of slate or black iron. The tunnel was like a splinter, like broken glass, the space left when the shard has fallen, a hammer crack, the moment when stone certainty breaks and is undone.

Yet as it wended deep, as the dark receded and enclosed behind, a patch of moss would return an emerald glow, a growth of crystal a spark, a vein of gold a gleam, a tracery in the hollow. The candle flame now bent and rose and bent and rose with steady gait, so Mikhaèl had to protect it with a cupped hand from guttering. Though its flame remained strong, the candle ungrew. The wax now covered Mikhaèl's hand in a warm clasp. The breath of the wind dashed tears from Mikhaèl's cheeks. There was a whisper on the wind, a distant song. As he picked his way around juttings of stone in the ruddy dark, of a sudden a cavern opened before him, vast.

Here from the walls crystal in great clumps and spears and flowerings caught the blue of the sky from an arch in the wall opposite. In the bowl of the hearth cave amidst a scattering, a cairn of ugly oilstones, misshapen, dull and scored and greasy, atop the mound a rock uglier still, red and smooth and dark.

As Mikhaèl passed toward the arch of blue, his shape caught gold and silver flickering in the glassy surfaces of each bloom of stone above, a rock of the cairn slid and tumbled, and another, and they all fell away as a great red ill-made man stood and took him in knot-raw hands like slabs of meat.

"I am the father of misery, the husband of stone. I am the lord of all that wearies, the king of all that rots, you have mastered my son and evaded my wife, but no one escapes my grasp, I am the breaker, I am the unmaker, from your quickness I take halt, from your halt I make mire, from your mire stone, from stone, dust, from dust, darkness and unknowing. Neither iron nor stone nor honour nor memory stands before me. I am The King Below The World, I will have your golden heart, so none shall remember."

"This cold thing in my chest? It is eternal. It shines and shines and the brightness of it gives me hurt. You may take it for any old lump of living stone. Promise that you will unhold me, and I will cut it out for you myself."

"May the world crack if you lie!"

"May it awake from ruin if do you."

A toll sounded at the bargain, because above riot and ruin, darkness and stone, each world above is made on the agreements of the world below.

Mikhaèl lay, opened his vest, and took the golden pinion that had slain his beloved in hand, held it poised above his chest. "Give me the stone," he said.

The King Unearth placed a rock in his hand.

"This is an ugly thing, and dull. You promised me a living stone." He cast it aside.

The King Unmaker placed a great flower of white crystal in his hand.

"This is a pretty thing, but cold. You promised me a living stone."

The King Breaker placed a great red ruby in his hand.

"This is a precious thing, but its fire is fleeting. You promised me a living stone."

"The fire of the sun shall light above the precipice in a moment. In that fire you shall see the ruby burn."

"A semblance. You promised me a living stone, or by our bargain the world will be made anew."

"The only stone here is my own mighty heart, that makes and unmakes all things. It is too great a thing for the likes of you."

"I can feel all that you have unmade tremble."

"Oh no, there is one other stone that will do."

The lumpen man took from Mikhaèl's vest the silver collide-o-scope, and broke it in twain.

The red monster grinned in glee. "I have unmade this union twice now. Here is your heart." And it placed the diadem in Mikhaèl's hand.

"You have paid for it, have it then."

With the tip of the golden pinion, Mikhaèl pierced his chest. The red man leaned above, chortling, Mikhaèl swung the blade so the creature scuttle back on its haunches. He reached in and pulled forth the golden heart and with a great sob cast it aside. He held the jewel above the hollow space in his chest and as the sun lit through the arch the diadem shone, and every stone and glass in the hearth cave flickered with the captured moment, before Mikhaèl took it as his heart. With melted wax from his hand he closed the wound. The creature in that brightness sobbed. Then all was dark.

The lumpen face with its eyes of coal peered out from the mound of oilstones. As Mikhaèl stood the pain in his chest speared and soothed.

"When the ice melts and the water rushes down the precipice you shall fall, broken on each water polished stone and not even a glowing heart will protect you." The thing was timid, cowed. Hiding.

Mikhaèl saw the wax in his chest, lit underneath golden white, like a winter sun.

"Why do you hide?"

"It hurts my eyes."

Mikhaèl closed his vest and tied it. It was chill any way.

"Here, I have hidden my light."

"Hide your light as you must, you cannot pass this precipice."

"That's a pretty tune, monster. Tell me a little more."

"Hide your light as you must,

Though you dance and make a fuss,

Nowt with wing nor omnibus,

You shall not pass this precipice."

Mikhaèl looked through the stone arch into the blue. The golden sun lit his eyes until he wept.

Below down sheer cliffs of black stone and sheet ice, was a bowl, darkly verdant, sheltered around by peaks hard and looming. From a ravine through the shoulders of two such a cataract fell, gem coloured, falling from empty heights through bare broken cliffs and mountain forests swathed in cloud to the wild green expanse so far below, where it meandered serpentine and vanished to where the world ended, where the sun's golden path lit upon the water.

In that distance, on the ocean's horizon, a spindle silver and gold and as high as the precipice rose into the sky. Golden cloud swirled around its height.

"You see! You see!" Cried the monster, rattling under his stones, so they clattered.

"Hide your love light as you must,
Though it burns within your breast,
Though you dance and beat you chest,
Though you win through every test,
Though you cry and make a fuss,
Nowt with wing nor omnibus,
You shall not pass this precipice."

"Prettier still. Unmaker, you have learned Making."

There was silence from under the stones. Then the lumpen creature's voice, tentative, "I have learned, may-king."

"Here, sing your song again. We shall make your song prettier still. Take up two stones and bang them together thusly. I'll show you. Sing your song! Sing your song!"

As the monster sang, Mikhaèl beat the rocks together, with each smash sparks flew.

"Now you! Now you!"

The monster leaped once more from his stone midden, grinned with ruby teeth, slammed his feet and crashed the rocks together sending out great sparks like lightning. Mikhaèl danced, with the beast drumming for all he was worth.

"Great Unmaker rubble and rust,
Little May King all but dust,
Hide your love light as you must,
Though it burns within your breast,
Though you dance and beat your chest,
Though you win through every test,
Though you cry and make a fuss,
Nowt with wings nor omnibus,
I'll grind your bones ere you rest,
You shall not pass this precipice."

The Lord of Dust fell to the ground laughing and hooting. Mikhaèl capered and danced humming the tune on the ledge above the blue.

"If only we had a pipe such as my son plays, what a pretty tune we could make!"

"Oh we have such. This ugly golden thing you took from me. As fine a pipe as ever was played. Blow us a tune and we'll make such a song and dance!"

The Misshapen One placed the golden heart to his mouth. "I am a thing of the Stone Before Time. I have neither lips nor breath. I cannot play it."

"Here. Lend it me and I shall play the pipe and you shall sing and drum and we shall have a merry song to make a man out of a monster."

"Play on! Play on!"

Mikhaèl placed the heart to his lips and blew; there echoed forth a sound like a great flute, at once deep and shining. He played a tune as a sailor would, a jig both merry and mournful, full of the joy of the sea and the longing for home. The monster danced and sang and drummed.

"Great Unmaker rubble and rust,
Little May King all but dust,
Hide your love light as you must,
Though it burns within your breast
Though you dance and beat your chest,
Though you win through every test,
Though you cry and make a fuss,
Nowt with wings nor omnibus,

I'll grind your bones ere you rest,
You shall not pass this precipice."
And the heart melted away to breath in Mikhaèl's
hands. Then the birds came. Great flocks of them,
swirling in flight, eagle and egret, robin and crow. They
seized Mikhaèl with claws in his vest and hair and skin,
and flew.

"The words of man, never trust!" shouted the
creature.

"Oh monster my friend, what is an *omnibus*?" called
Mikhaèl.

But though the monster stood at the ledge
shouting, the birds had carried Mikhaèl too far, and the
buffeting of their wings was too loud, to hear the King
of Dust's reply.

As he descended, so the floor of the valley
changed from tangled abundance to riot. Amid the
thorny vines bearing plump fruits and the bobbing
heads of poppy and violet nettle, grew gnarled woody
knots, their branches thick with red and orange fruits.
On taller trees, great green and conical, towering
trunks bore spreading branches, spacious and even.
Amidst sprays of needles hung dark cones, about
which birds busied themselves, taking the seeds from
within to nests hidden in the lower canopy. Taller still,

great white trunks with sparse arms, leaves in russet and yellow and brown like thick spread hands. Here birds red and blue like plumes of fire sat calling a high chatter, chirping and preening.

The flock that gathered him up set Mikhaèl down amidst the warm jungle. With much speech and bobbing of heads they brought him soft feathered slippers, red and blue, and a cloak of plumes, grey as a dove, they brought him flower trumpets, full of sweet water, and ripe and pungent fruit, and then in a flurry they departed.

Mikhaèl ate the red fruit, which was sweet like a peach but tart like an apple, and quenched his thirst with flower water, then he wrapped himself in the dove grey cloak and slept. While he slept he heard a high and pretty song, distant but calling.

When he woke he put the fiery slippers to his feet, and made a peaked helm of the fruit's hard rind. He took his golden sword in hand, and set off through the Birdswood. As he travelled his feathered feet lit lightly over branch and limb, earth and mire, stone and water. Rivulets passed under his feet as easy as paths, ravines he leapt like they were cracks in the pavement. As he went on the skin of his shoes calloused and hardened. His stone bird shoes flew nevertheless.

One morning he woke in the golden mist, the birdsong quiet for a moment, the forest canopy above still emerald dark, and a vine of red flowers had grown through his beard.

He came to the gem like river, all crystal blue and foaming white, and strode from wave tip to wave tip like an acrobat leaping from back to back on fleet charging horses.

Glimpses of the tower showed through leaves and tangles, all black stone and silver glass and gleaming gold. Soon the canopy thinned to skeletal branches amid a thorny bracken, both bare of fruit and leaf, then fields of sallow grass and boulders, then moors of moss and nettle and heather, and still the river charged on.

Where it turned to cascade and thunder over the edge of the world and down to the endless sea, a white mist filled the air.

The tower now rose like a carnival bauble, now jewel, now candy. Its turret above the golden clouds like a carved poppy, or bishop's crown, a rose or rose hip. Petals gaurdant, a flower enclosed. Or a glass heart; easily broken.

And what from a distance had once been a glass tower was now a glass mountain. Around its base lay all manner of dead birds, some their whole bodies frozen gold in poses of flight, others a carcass with a gold wing or talon, these twisted out of shape, still others gold skulls joined supine bones, and all around wing and bone and skull and rib cage were scattered piecemeal everywhere.

Mikhaèl watched for a day. Birds great and small would flock up to the mountain's sculpted peak, many bearing fruit and flowers as Mikhaèl had seen them do himself. What heartless creature called their tune? The birds would take wing, back to nests and roosts. A song distant, sad and as empty as spun gold would echo from the peak. Birds would fall, hitting the soft earth heavily, turned in part or whole to bright metal. As evening fell the sun quenched in the unending ocean, lit gold and fire on the peak and the clouds. Through the night the mountain gleamed with a fey light.

In the morn Mikhaèl called to the birds, but without a heart to charm them they paid him no heed. So he set to climbing, taking up two great golden talons as grapples which bit into the jewelled skin of the mountain, and where he kicked his stone bird feet into the glass it starred and gave him purchase.

He climbed and climbed, over petal, spiral, icicle and unmoving cataract. On sheer faces he slid and fell, and struck toes and claws deep into the glass, muscles burning and heart glowing. In other places a maze of curlicues and protuberances saw him climbing crab-wise, this way and that, so that the mountain surface now seemed merely an over complicated ground, gravity only weariness. As night and birds fell, he found a cup and cupola in red, like an orchid, its bowl filled with only a little gold, where he sheltered.

The following day he climbed up and up. Here so many layers and rivulets of spun gold and glass made the climb easy. Up and up, through chill white cloud mist and drifts warm and golden. Here his cloak and even his skin took a golden hue. Now the chamber at the top of the mountain loomed. Here, at this great height was ice and glass. Each grip was treacherous.

This evening he found a ledge like a frozen pond, icicles spreading from its sides in sprays. The singing voice was now clear and almost familiar, sad but comforting, like the song of a gentle nurse, remembered from childhood. The air was golden with the song, it entranced and drew him on. At night the weeping also, though the strength of it was something inhuman.

His heart ached through the night, so he climbed before even the sun lit above the peaks. The birds flew and fell, and clinging for dear life he came up and over the parapet.

Here a girl with golden eyes and skin like cream and hair like night's wings, blue black and full of diadems, dressed in tangled finery, stepped forth and placed a golden pear to his lips. Mikhaèl was overwrought, he cried and shrieked, that this beauteous thing had killed his lest love, and bellowed, "Girl with the voice worth its weight in gold, will you sing for me?"

"Oh great parrot, tell your cruel Master I will not sing for him him until the day he tells me my name. Alas he has no voice to tell me who I am, and you have no heart to speak, except his cold litany. I sing and weep, but not for you, thoughtless bird, or your cruel King."

Angered, Mikhaèl flew at the girl, shrieking. The heat of it was so great, the wax in his chest melted. The diadem fell from the raw cavity and disappeared amongst a thousands shards of broken glass. Mikhaèl struck her face with a talon, tearing her cheek and ugly mouth.

"Oh I have a name for you, and your cruel spell, I know well the song you sing with your voice that is worth its weight in gold, but I will never tell."

And he cast himself from the parapet, toward the blinding gold of the sun, and the birds took him up, and carried him down.

Fish-child

There once was a fishwife of a worn to silver seaside town, who, though her hands were stung by years of scales and salt, was nevertheless admired, her hair the ink and spindrift of the sea at night, her smile changeable as tides.

Each day her husband, a brown and knotted driftwood man, would return in his coracle with two baskets of fish. Those with melancholy eyes she salted, those with iridescent skin she cut and quartered for the traders who carried such bounty to places far and strange. Some she smoked and put aside for their own larder, and some she prepared with herbs and roots for their evening meal.

The sea was generous, offering fish and sometimes curious storm washed things, and though their days were unchanging, for the most part they were content. Except – except, though they coupled most nights, the way the sea and shore did, still, they had no child. Sometimes she felt as bare as the tideline on those moonless, silent winter mornings, when the sea had scoured, and receded.

One evening when she could hear the quiet susurr of mothers in nearby houses singing to their children, she remembered what her grandmother had told her when she was young, in a time of famine. "Carve a bone so it will float, a stone so it will sink, and a knuckle entwined between. Cast it in the deep at sunset, and sit vigil through the night on the empty shore. Light no fire, sing no songs. Sometime before the dawn, the octopus headed god will come ashore. Ask of that stranger your boon." She remembered two hungry seasons, and how they ended in sudden wealth from the sea, and that her grandmother after each had shortened fingers on her sinister hand.

Thus, in the dark of a midsummer eve, when her husband followed the season's night shoals with the other men, she carved a blue-green stone the shape of an eye, and a knob of bone into a hollow like a cup, and she cut the smallest finger from her hand, pressing the blade in at the first phalanx the way she sometimes separated the leg bones of a fowl. Her tears were more of determination than of pain.

She tied the pieces together, clumsy fingers bloodying the string, so that the nub of flesh, already no longer part of her, but just the bait necessary for a very particular fish, sat equally between the cup and weight. She bandaged her hand in salve and ribbon, and went to the shore, uncertain, of the ache in her hand, or belly, or heart, which was worse.

She swung the lure above her head, the hole in the stone whistling, and let it fly, and it flew far out beyond the night-limned lazy breakers, to where the sea was calm and black and shot through with luminescence. The bone cup floated on the surface, the way palace flowers floated in an ornamental pond in a painting she had seen. The morsel floating somewhere in the layer of brightness could not be told. The stone hung below, in the dark.

She sat on the sand, and pulled her shawl tighter, forgetting her injury for a moment, til it stung. She thought of a child, challenging and retreating from the waves. Of a golden haired boy, trimming a triangular sail. Of a driftwood man, like but unlike her husband, holding his own child in his arms.

The bone flower bobbed, and vanished below the black waters. Green swirled where it had been. Then with a sound like leather, something, someone, emerged from the sea. He had the aspect a of silver skinned youth in a coral crown, and at once, a gnarled and barnacled deepdweller, slow of eye, sudden of sting.

"Woman, do you hunger?" said the creature, with a sound like waves spilling from lipless mouth, hair writhing.

"Oh I hunger."

"I have tasted, and know your hunger.'

A great salamander, glistening, blotched and pale, crawled out of the waters behind the sea god. At the sight of it her mouth turned hard, and her breasts warmed and ached.

"Take this child of the sea, do not speak of it, but care for it as you would your own, and in seven years come back to me, and you will, of your flesh and blood, have a child of your own."

Tears wet her face as she scooped the thing up in her shawl and held it against her breast. It made a mewling sound and she felt small soft fingers on her skin, grasping her nipple.

"Mama," it said, and fed as she fled home.

"Wife, I am the fisherman, yet you bring me a fish," laughed her husband, home from his labours, as she walked into the kitchen. "Shall I be the fishwife then? Put it on the bench and I will gut it for you. Though I must say, this beast makes a rank oil, and an ill meat, though I warrant its sharp teeth make a vicious scourge."

"With that beard and those clumsy hands you make a poor fishwife, my dear. Perhaps a fish-husband? I have heard tell these creatures turn from fish to firedrake under a red moon, with flames for plumage, that I would have for my new midsummer's festival dress, so I will keep it awhile."

"We shall be the talk of the town, the wife who keeps a fish wrapped in a shawl like a swaddling! Well, keep your ugly fish. When he has grown shall we make a feast or send him to the minster to learn his letters?"

"If he wants, to learn his letters, he will," she said.

The creature in her arms burbled with a sound like the sea against the sides of hollow boats, a peculiarly contented laughter.

The household soon settled into a routine. Thorgold, who was a kindly man, and believed there were still greater mysteries in the sea than fish that walked and wives that pined, brought into the house an old oak bath. He caulked it well with pith and gum, filled it with sand and rocks and seawater, so it made its own little shore, where the creature could bask on the sand or partially submerged in the brine, as was his wont.

Anwen, (for that was the fish-mother's name) set to knitting a cardigan of coloured wool in a thick rope pattern, which would hold moisture well. Young Oompla made mewling complaint if he slept too close to the fire and his skin dried. The sea damp cardigan kept his skin iridescent and gleaming, and he would burble, "Oompla" quite contentedly. By a kind of natural, unspoken agreement, all three quickly recognised this sound, like small waves against a wooden hull, as the creature's name.

"Oommpla, my dear, come to the table for your supper," Anwen would sing in the evening, and Oompla would burble "Oompla", and come from his tub on skinny, dexterous legs, to sit at the table and eat his favourite, steamed white bait and sea greens. After he would smile with a wide, toothsome grin.

Later in the evening, Thorgold would show Oompla the tying of knots and other sea crafts, and with his small nimble fingers, Oompla was proficient after only a few tries, while Anwen read poems and stories from *The Book Of The Sea*, to which husband and child would both respond with exclamations of "Oooom!", at the exciting feats and monstrous discoveries, and "Plaaaaaaaa," at the terrible tempests and tragic drownings.

There were many busy words spoken behind idle hands when Anwen would take Oompla, wearing his cardigan and wrapped in a net sling against her chest to market. To such empty-lipped looks and scandalised questions she would just say that she was bringing up a fish for his midsummer plumage, no more, no less, and that was the end of the matter.

Well, the end, until, after several weeks, a delegation of the town's concerned folk knocked at their door.

Anwen was stitching knotted appliqué anchors to a sea blue velvet coat she had made for Oompla, while the fish-child, with a few deft twists was tying more of the decorations. She stood, gathering Oompla in his net sling, behind her.

The village master, perhaps part walrus, stood in their small parlour, kindly frowning, and the priest, at least as much lammergeier as lordling, bent below the low figured ceiling, where tools and lamps and gourds and drying fish and herbs and bobs of coloured glass hung from scraps of net, spoke.

"The folk are concerned, Anwen, if this is a fish, or a child. It is said even the Lord and the high folk in his great hall laugh at the idiot village where the women have fish rather than bairns." Those gathered outside the open door, nodded and grumbled in assent, the sky behind them darkening in the bruised colours of a fast approaching summer squall.

"Fools will always frown or laugh," Anwen replied, "but I'm sure his lordship has bigger fish to fry." Oompla, from her back, peered cautiously over.

"As *The Book Of The Sea* says, 'Keep of the sea what the sea freely gives, return to the sea what belongs to the sea'," fiercely quoth the priest.

"I hear tell the Emperor of Malagasy has a golden fish with curling moustaches, that his seven concubines feed sweetmeats everyday, and that he augurs from its fast flickering movements his plans for conquest, but this is no such fish as that, this is a plain fish, out of water I grant you, but still quite spry and plump. Of course it is said such fish grant long-life and renewed vigour when reduced to a broth, but if that is your aim I tell you, sirs, when the sea gives you such a fish, you may have it, but this fish is my fish."

"And yet, Anwen, you carry the creature, and burble to it, and dress it in fine raiment," said the priest, the apple in his throat bobbing in a manner both reviling and voracious.

"I hear the Lord, when a child, had a bear that wore a vest and doublet, knew its own name and could count to three. Did the Lord's folk make demands of his mother that the bear be turned loose in the woods for sport, or drained of its bile to invigorate their lax appendages? I think not."

"Ah, exactly then, Anwen. If this fish that you carry as a child can speak his name, and count his numbers, he must be both baptised and attend school for his letters, if not, the village will decide if it shall be consumed by all in a healthful broth, or returned to the sea."

About then the rising squall struck. Those outside wetting their lips fled at the downpour, clutching at escaping hats and the lapels of their flax coats. The priest stood glowering.

Oompla said, "Oompla," and squirted the crowing man with three quick squirts of water from his full gullet pouches, counting gleefully in his chirrupy voice, "One, two, three!" after each briny squirt.

"It has been decided, then," the village master said, beaming. "Young Oompla shall be baptised and learn his trades and letters with the other village children."

The priest dabbed gloweringly at his face with a linen kerchief, while Anwen laughed and held Oompla close, and thought to the bargain she made on the beach, and what that sea god would think of its fosterling learning *hey-ho-a-day* and three plus three, and joinery, and to sew a shark skin jerkin and cast a weighted net, and all the other lore of those who live above the sea in its graces, not below it.

Oompla was baptised in rainwater and in salt, as was the custom, from a driftwood bowl, by the whalebone temple on the shore, the villages singing songs of praise from *The Book* to the new child. What they thought, who knew, but some remembered the squall of the day it was decided, and the blue calm of the morning of the ceremony, and took it as a portent.

In the upturned hull that served as kirkroom and school, Oompla soon learned that he could calculate on his sixteen lithe toes and fingers more rapidly than the other children on their ten. Although the sea-sough and basso waves of his voice were not readily given to debate, or history, or argument, or the other flimsy arts, he could sing two countered parts from *The Book Of The Sea* in contrasting harmonies to great effect, earning in equal measure suspicion and respect from Father Urgolain. While the children played games of *Cast The Net*, and *Rover, Red Rover*, on the sand when the priest attended some other duty, Oompla showed them how he could call waves, a little faster and higher, with his sea voice, and once, when one small group of boys got it in their stern jaws and stony knuckles to punish him for his soft and glimmering appearance, and held him down and roughed his appliquéd jacket, he called a roil of green crabs from the coral reefs, that swarmed up and pinched the boys, vicious with hard, serrated pincers, until they howling fled. Oompla called calming waves to ease the crabs' way back to their domain, this song calmed the children too, and from then he would sing it quietly if the children grew hard and sharp and brittle, as they seemed to do when gathered in vying crowds.

Despite the scowls of the priest, his glaring fish-hawk aspect, Anwen walked Oompla to the school's shell blazoned door each day, and meet him there again in the early afternoon.

"Were the other children cruel today?" she would ask, "Was Father Urgolain?"

"No, Mother, I sang him the song of the Red Tern, from *The Book*, and he was pleased, and I showed the children how the narwhals joust like knights, and they were pleased. Jesma said she liked my coat, I showed her your way of tying string in fish and fronds and anchors for its decoration."

Oompla both learned his lessons and grew faster than the other children, and in the span of a few bountiful seasons sat at the back of the class, with the older children, given less to play and more to the tasks demanded of passing time. His mother had made him a fine new sea-silk coat, and Jesma had made him a necklet of knotted glass and anchors. She had eyes like the summer sea, and the summer's furious laughter. He had grown into a handsome walking fish, upright as a voyager, with coloured patterns on his skin like the words of God. To see them walking through the market, or calling waves like stallions on the shore, was to imagine the young gods had come again amongst them.

But one morning when he went to meet her by the arced bones of the sea temple, she was not there. At the polished ebon door of her father's house, a servant through the latch simply said, "She is no longer here." When Oompla insisted, in his sea voice, her father came, bearing a harpoon, a drunken, squalling aspect, and said, "Begone, creature."

The sea rose and the day darkened. At home his mother said, "She has gone to serve on one of the great Lord's ships, using the sea songs you taught her to call kind winds and easing waves. Your friendship has brought her much honour, and she would be here if she could."

"In the great deep of the sea, hours slow to days, days to years. The great leviathan's heart strikes only once in a handful of moments, but with as much love as any mother for her sea-lost child. I think I will return to the sea, mother, for time, here, now, has become so much more burdensome than that weight, my heart has stopped."

"Soon my love," Anwen said. The nub of her small finger had been aching again of late. The seventh midsummer was fast approaching.

It was a moonless night, the polished sea softly singing, the other folk had turned home, from their celebrations. Around some dimming fires, others slept away the gleam and raucous laughter of their intoxicated dreams.

Anwen, holding Oompla's small cool hand, walked to the quiet, stony beach around the heads, beyond the sea-temple, where the receding tide exposed a scape of frown and molten rock, black and coally hissing.

From the steam and roil of one eye-dark pool, the sea-god rose, water pouring off his green and mottle skin like blue flame from burning copper.

"You have fattened this creature for seven years, kept it in health," the deep one said, in that now familiar voice of wave and cliff, "preserved its life from threat, nurtured it through its changes. Revealed nought of this bargain. Now it is grown. You may cast it in these burning stones, and consume each morsel of its flesh, then, in months hence, you will be with child, or, for the offering of another morsel from your hand, you may take the creature, and for another seven years, return home."

The sea god held forth a knife, jewelled and barnacled, the crescent blade honed and bill-hook bright.

Anwen thought of that child, of that young driftwood man, nut brown, sea-polished, with his own sand-coloured child in his arms, and of this wide-mouthed, lantern-eyed creature, with its fleshy moustaches, and silvery, ink blemished skin, its laments, sea songs and laughter.

Oompla looked at her, an oil-thick tear silking from the corner of his eye.

She thought; this was the first time she had seen him cry.

"Oh, Mama," Oompla said.

Taking the knife from the sea-god's hand, she did.

Mirrors & Slivers

The Starspikes are so tall as to cause one to imagine that, from space, they must appear as a beard of icicles depending like an old man's goatee from the round face of the Earth. But, of course, they are not so tall. Still, the mirrored, three sided spikes ascend so high that, on clear days ball lightning gathers around their tips, curious sparkling entities that discharge to earth in a violent flash that runs the length of the spike.

And when the big storms that scour the surface of the Earth rush over, the tips of the spikes score green iridescent streaks in the soft underbelly of the cloud. On these stormy days the mirrored sides of the spikes boil with the storm's reflected, swirling darkness.

When lightning strikes amongst the forest of spikes its momentary illumination is re-reflected and multiplied so that hours later, in the stillness after the passing of the storm, before the *Aurora Tempestuosus* envelopes the evening with its spectral shimmerings, the lightning can still be seen, dancing amongst the spikes.

Rigelspike is launching today. It is more than the lightning of storms past, trapped within that gold-tinted sliver, that today draws our eyes toward it.

The mirrors of this city (for it is now merely that; there is no longer any escape velocity to defy the Earth's thickening gravity) seemingly ascend further into the sky with each passing week. Of course, this too is illusion. Maybe it is only our own increasing burden that makes the spikes seem, on a calm autumn day like today, so much more towering.

Though fractured on the surfaces of the Starspikes, each reflecting back the sky coloured by its own hues, creating a jagged and multiple horizon, the blue space and cloud mottle reduced and captured there is ordered too.

It's curious, each workday I ascend those structures and descend their outer surfaces, yet from here, on the edge of the ruined metropolis where we Grounders live, they seem so alien, so unfamiliar. I'm not really suited to my employ as a window washer; I think too much about falling. That doesn't scare me, though. I see the gulls and the pigeons still defying gravity, wheel in the strange high places between Starspikes, they traverse those empty geometries so easily, I sometimes imagine that I would too.

Up there the air hums, the noise of traffic below is little more than background static, and when the wind that precedes a storm soughs in, its currents pull at you and you feel the Starspike sway.

I watch myself in those enormous lying mirrors, and watch my self's image blur with soapy water when I sponge, and materialize with such disturbing clarity when I squeegy.

At certain conjunctions of space and light I glimpse my tertiary, my quaternary, and higher orders of selves transformed and reflected back that occasionally I wonder if in fact that distant person deep within the glass is not some other yellow coveralled and capped window washer who merely delights in mimicry of me.

No it is not the prospect of falling to the ground, that toy landscape, that scares me, but falling into myself in that infinite space...that fear grips me and sends my imagination reeling so I must stare and stare into myself, into glimpses of those deeper selves, to ride out that vertiginous fear.

Up there the clouds drift by so close I could easily be seduced by their materiality to step out, but only into the glass. I prefer not to wear a harness when I'm out in the cradle, though Silverman, my supervisor, insists I must, guild rules and insurance clauses. Nor am I supposed to work alone but Silverman has, in his twenty years of cleaning and remirroring the spikes, developed an assortment of voyeuristic liaisons which he relishes in describing to me. So, as soon as he has seen me buckled into my harness and left for just such a perverse meeting, I unbuckle and hang precariously over the cradle rail, laughing and crying out in sheer defiance. Such are the petty amusements we perform in defiance of gravity, to assert our freedom.

On chill mornings I often drive the cradle directly where the sun blazes in the glass, and revel there in ecstatic luminance, suspended in my harness. Such enlightenment, when I blink open my watering eyes and glimpse my reflected self within that blazing orb, Icarus triumphant in heliolatry, is beyond understanding.

Once, while driving the cradle horizontally across a spike for just such an exultant self-apotheosis the sun exploded outwards and a chair fell in a rain of glittering shards. A man quickly followed and I noticed his smile. The hole left in that infinity was a jagged edged blackness.

On certain shrouded days, when my primary reflection is little more than a ghost, I can see the adumbrate figures behind the glass. So empty, the orderly toings and froings of these shades, trapped by mirrors and screens and glass in the line of sight hierarchy that makes a spike a functional organism, broken only when they notice me noticing them and they pull faces and perform curious motionings to see how well I see them. Of course, I act oblivious to their gestures and they find themselves, observed by their hierarchical superior, acting the fool. These are the only times, it seems, they pause, as I, to reflect.

But today no doubt many of them are reflecting. The Pinnacle of Rigelspike has commanded an attempt to launch. The last such attempt occurred seventeen years ago, when I was three. My family deserted Proximaspike and became Grounders only that morning.

To my three year old eyes it was a beautiful thing to see; that sliver reflecting the yellow dawn lift itself up above the other spikes so that it blazed golden in the sun, before exploding in a downpour of prismatic daggers.

Of course, gravity has grown so much heavier since then.

So we Grounders in our bright coloured coveralls and caps watch from the edge of the deserted metropolis, and a young family, deserting Rigelspike, their meagre possessions packed in an electric car, crosses the cement field toward us. Beyond the black and yellow striped checkpoint without looking back.

They arrive at our small celebration.

"Hi. I'm Daniel Windows," I say. "Welcome back to Earth."

"Why are you crying, Daniel Windows?" their child asks me.

"These mirrors are a curious sad wounding of time, and of space. For everything that is beautiful and futile, and everything that is tragic and purposeful. For these mirrors, aspiring to the night. Don't you see, my eyes are laughing also."

And we watch Rigelspike rise trembling into the blue. And there is as much laughter, as tears in their eyes, but only wonder in the eyes of their child.

About The Author

C S Hughes grew up on the fringes of Australia's dust blown towns and salt blown cities. He claims he was a hobo in his youth, and later worked as a spice seller, a book dealer, a watch repairer, and a trader in junk and assorted detritus.

More recently he has been a writer and publisher of poetry books, (by way of madness rather than vocation), editing *From The Ashes - Poetry In Support Of Bushfire Relief*, *The Poetry Of John Ashdown-Hill* and *Somnia Blue,* amongst others. He curates the site hooliganstreetpoetry.org, has been published online and in print in *Blue Pepper, Five 2 One*, *Weird Tales, Sampietrino, The Blue Nib* and various others. He has published several collections of his own work, including, *The Little Book Of Funerals, The Book Of Whimsies, The Book Of Barbarous Tales*, and the novella in verse, *COVID-22*.

He currently lives in the Gippsland Lakes region of Victoria with a cat and an historian, where he studies and dabbles in story writing, but claims, with a nearly straight face, to still mostly being a hobo.